THE MAGIC ROUNDABOUT

MR MACHENRY'S INVENTION

Story by Helen Lloyd
Illustrations by Primary Design

Mr MacHenry was in an inventing mood, but he needed some inspiration…

"I'll go and talk to Dougal and Florence. I'm sure they will help me," he said to himself.

When Mr MacHenry arrived, Florence was organising paper chains, but Dougal wasn't getting on very well.

"Yow! What's all this about anyway?" he grumbled.

"It's a surprise party for Mr Rusty," said Florence.
"It's his birthday today, but he hasn't told anyone."

Mr MacHenry watched as Dougal got into an even bigger mess with his paper chains.

"Now, that gives me an idea," said Mr MacHenry.
"I'll see you at the party." He wandered off,
muttering to himself.

"We won't see him for hours," said Dougal.
"These inventors are always the same – never around
when you want something really useful."

When the decorations were ready, Florence asked
Zebedee about party food.
"I'll do what I can," he said.

Jelly, cake and sandwiches appeared on the table.
"That's wonderful, Zebedee," said Florence.
"I'll fetch Mr Rusty now."

"How did you know it was my birthday?"
asked Mr Rusty.
"Don't ask me," said Brian. "This was Florence's idea."

"That was very thoughtful of you, my dear.
Thank you," said Mr Rusty.

In his inventing shed, Mr MacHenry was just finishing his invention.

"Perfect! Now I can show it to everyone," he said.
"I hope they've saved me some party food –
inventing is hungry work!"

Mr MacHenry arrived just as Florence gave
Mr Rusty a box.
"This is your birthday present," she said.

Mr Rusty opened the box.
"That's just what I need!" he said. "A new
feather for my hat."

"Sorry I'm late," said Mr MacHenry. "It took me a long time to finish my invention."

Dougal tried not to look interested.
"What is it, what does it do?" asked Brian, who was.

"I'll show you," said Mr MacHenry.
Carefully, he put the box and Mr Rusty's old feather
in the machine.

"Then I press this button," he explained.

The machine whirred and flowers came out from
the other end of the machine.
"My rubbish convertor can make something new
out of all our rubbish," said Mr MacHenry
proudly.

"Now, is there any food left for me?"
"Oops!" said Dougal, looking at the empty table.

Florence looked at Zebedee and soon Mr MacHenry had some food.

"What an exciting birthday for Mr Rusty," said Florence. "A party and an invention for us all!"

THE EXPEDITION

Story by Helen Lloyd
Illustrations by Primary Design

When Dougal arrived at the Magic Roundabout,
Mr Rusty was upset.
"What's the matter?" asked Dougal.

"Look!" cried Mr Rusty. "One of my roundabout horses is missing! Where can it be?"

"Hmm," said Dougal, thinking to himself.
"This will take a good deal of brains and cunning,"
he said in a loud voice. "I'll organise a search party."

"I'll come with you," said Mr Rusty. "But who will make sure the others are safe while I'm away?"

"I will," said Brian. "I'll guard them for you."

Florence joined the search party.
"I always have good ideas," she said.

Dylan had just fallen asleep as usual.
"You won't get out of it that easily," said Dougal.

They split up into pairs to search all over
the garden.

"Make sure you keep that rabbit awake,"
said Dougal, as Florence set off with Dylan.

Dougal and Mr Rusty went to the quietest corner
of the garden.
"Can you hear someone talking?" whispered Dougal.

Dougal and Mr Rusty crept closer so that they could peep through the trees.

"Now dear, what about this one?" Ermintrude was saying. "It looks jolly delicious, don't you think?"

"My horse!" said Mr Rusty.

"Thank you for looking after my horse, Ermintrude,"
said Mr Rusty. "Where did you find it?"
Ermintrude went a little pinker than usual.

"Well, I thought it looked dizzy going round on the roundabout all day. So I brought it here with me."
"I don't believe this," muttered Dougal.

"The problem is, dear," she continued, "I can't get it to show an interest in eating anything."

"It's a roundabout horse, Ermintrude," said Mr Rusty.
"It likes giving Florence and the others rides.
It doesn't need to eat like a normal horse."

Dylan and Florence had decided to search the
quietest corner of the garden too.
"You've found the horse!" said Florence. "Oh, good."

"Let's take it back straight away," said Dougal.
"Before Ermintrude has any more ideas."

Gently, they put the horse back on the roundabout.

Then Mr Rusty played a tune on the barrel organ.
Ermintrude watched as all the horses went
round and round.

"You were right, Mr Rusty," she said. "But I'm sure my horse looks better for its little adventure, don't you agree, Dougal?"

DYLAN'S DISGUISE

Story by Helen Lloyd

Illustrations by Primary Design

Dylan was learning a new song on his guitar. Things weren't going too well – in fact Dylan had just started to snore when Brian and Dougal arrived.

"I've got an idea," hissed Dougal. "Watch this!"

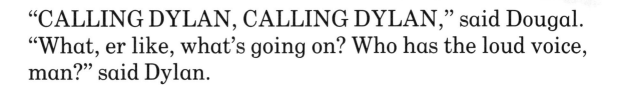

"CALLING DYLAN, CALLING DYLAN," said Dougal. "What, er like, what's going on? Who has the loud voice, man?" said Dylan.

Then he noticed something in front of him.
"Far out," said Dylan. "Are you from another galaxy,
or am I still dreaming?"

Then Dylan heard giggling from behind the trees. "Hey guys, that wasn't very nice," he said.

"But it was very funny!" giggled Brian.
Dylan was almost cross. He picked up his guitar and
ambled off towards his vegetable patch.

"Psst!" said Ermintrude. "I couldn't help seeing that silly trick Dougal and Brian played on you, dear. I have an idea to play a little trick of your own!"

She pointed at some old clothes and told Dylan her plan.
"Great idea," grinned Dylan.

Later that day, someone new arrived in the garden. He wore strange clothes, and an even stranger hat, but he seemed very interesting.

"Hello," said Florence. "Welcome to the
Magic Garden."
"He reminds me of someone," whispered Brian.

First, the stranger painted a picture of Florence.
Then he did lots of other paintings.
"Why don't you make an exhibition of your paintings
in the garden?" said Florence.

"Oh, control yourself," said Dougal. "All this
attention will go to his head, whoever he is."

The exhibition was a great success.
"This one is my favourite," said Ermintrude.

"Thank you so much, dear."
She gave Dylan a huge wink.

"What else can you do?" asked Florence.
"Well, I can play lots of musical instruments,"
said the stranger.

So they asked him to do a concert.

After playing the drums and the trombone,
the stranger picked up his guitar.

"It's a pity that rabbit is missing this," said Dougal.
"I suppose he's asleep under a tree somewhere."

Then Dougal looked hard at the stranger. Brian was right. He did remind him of someone!
"I'll have you know I am considered a trombone virtuoso," said Dougal, getting on the stage.

"Dougal 'Angel Slide' Junior taught me all I know.
Can we do a duet?"
"Why sure," said the stranger.

When no one was looking, Dougal used the trombone to dislodge the hat. "Heh, heh," laughed Dougal. "Dylan, it's you!" said everyone.

"Typical of a rabbit!" muttered Dougal. "I hope you're all grateful to me for exposing this feeble trick!"

"Well, I think we should say thank you to Dylan," said Ermintrude. "He's really so talented, dears." "You're right," said Zebedee. "Hooray for Dylan!" Dougal was speechless.

Everyone turned round to give Dylan a round of applause. But he hadn't heard a word Ermintrude or Zebedee had said. He was fast asleep!

Stories first published in Great Britain 1992
by William Heinemann Ltd
an imprint of Reed Children's Books
Michelin House, 81 Fulham Road, London SW3 6RB
and Auckland, Melbourne, Singapore and Toronto
This edition first published 1994 by Dean
copyright © Reed International Books Ltd 1994
Magic Roundabout copyright © Serge Danot/AB Productions
Licensed by Link Licensing

Mr MacHenry's Invention copyright © Reed International Books Ltd 1992
The Expedition copyright © Reed International Books Ltd 1992
Dylan's Disguise copyright © Reed International Books Ltd 1992

ISBN 0 603 55374 5

Produced by Mandarin Offset
Printed and bound in China